DESTRUCTION
IN THE DESERT

DESTRUCTION IN THE DESERT

AN UNOFFICIAL MINECRAFTERS TIME TRAVEL ADVENTURE

BOOK THREE

Winter Morgan

Sky Pony Press
New York

Copyright © 2019 by Hollan Publishing, Inc.

Minecraft® is a registered trademark of Notch Development AB.

The Minecraft game is copyright © Mojang AB.

Sky Pony Press books may be purchased in bulk at special discounts for sales promotion, corporate gifts, fund-raising, or educational purposes. Special editions can also be created to specifications. For details, contact the Special Sales Department, Sky Pony Press, 307 West 36th Street, 11th Floor, New York, NY 10018 or info@skyhorsepublishing.com.

Sky Pony® is a registered trademark of Skyhorse Publishing, Inc.®, a Delaware corporation.

Minecraft® is a registered trademark of Notch Development AB.
The Minecraft game is copyright © Mojang AB.

Visit our website at www.skyponypress.com.

10 9 8 7 6 5 4 3 2

Library of Congress Cataloging-in-Publication Data is available on file.

Cover design by Brian Peterson
Cover illustration by Megan Miller

Print ISBN: 978-1-5107-3737-2
Ebook ISBN: 978-1-5107-3742-6

Printed in the United States of America

TABLE OF CONTENTS

1

GAME ON!

The list of rules was short. There were only two.

"What are the rules again?" asked Joe.

"Seriously?" Poppy shrugged, her brown braids fell onto her shoulders, and she readjusted her glasses. "The rules are that nobody gets hurt and that we all have fun."

Poppy, Joe, and Brett were in the last stages of planning a practical joke competition. They stood in the spacious living room in Poppy's new house she had designed. The project took Poppy a long time, and she was happy to have her friends Laura and Callie help her design and construct the house. She had built two extra bedrooms for her two builder friends. Poppy wanted them to stay with her when they visited Meadow Mews. Both Callie and Laura were participating in the competition, and Poppy was happy to have them as her guests in the large wooden home with a picture window overlooking the verdant landscape of Meadow Mews. The town farm, which Brett and Joe had constructed, could be seen in the distance.

Joe stared out the window and looked at the farm. He recalled the first time he met Poppy and Brett. He was summoned to work on a farm with Brett. After a few months of enjoying his new friends and new job, he decided to relocate from Farmer's Bay to Meadow Mews. Poppy helped him build a small stone house. It was down the road from Brett's house, and his window had a direct view of the farm. Joe loved waking up and looking out the window at the farm.

Although Joe loved his friends dearly, there was one aspect of the friendship that often bothered him. Ever since Joe met Brett and Poppy, he was aware of their constant pranking. Brett and Poppy were known pranksters, but now they wanted Joe to join in. Joe wasn't sure he wanted to pull a prank on anyone.

"I'm not sure I want to participate," said Joe.

Brett explained, "You have to join us, it will be fun."

Poppy added, "This is our first annual practical joke competition, and we really want you to be in it. Nancy and Helen are also taking part in the competition. Callie and Laura are arriving soon, too, because they're also competing."

"You can list a million people who are participating, but that doesn't mean I want to be in it," said Joe.

"But—" Poppy was about to list another reason Joe should participate when he cut her off.

"You can't peer pressure me," said Joe.

Brett said, "We don't want you to do anything you don't want to do."

"Yes," said Poppy. "If you really don't want to play a practical joke on anyone, we understand."

Brett's eyes widened. "I have a great idea. Why don't you judge the contest? You can decide who pulled the best joke."

"That's a good idea," said Joe. "I don't mind watching you guys pull pranks, but I don't like doing them myself."

"Great," Poppy said as Helen and Nancy walked into Poppy's living room. "Helen, Nancy!" she called out. "Joe is going to judge the practical joke competition."

As Poppy spoke, Callie and Laura arrived. Poppy was thrilled to have all of her friends at her house and ready to start the practical joke competition.

Laura said, "I have a really fun prank. I can't wait to play it on someone. When does the competition begin?"

Poppy replied, "Since everyone is here, we should start now. As you all know, this is the first year we are having the competition. Joe is going to judge it. There aren't any awards to hand out," she reminded them. "This is just a fun way to spend the day."

Joe said, "Your reward is knowing that I think you pulled the best prank."

"When is it over?" asked Laura.

"Tonight," said Poppy. "Everyone should be done with their pranks, and we will meet back here to go over what we pulled. Also, the two major rules of the competition are to have fun and to make sure nobody gets hurt during a prank."

"Smart rules," said Callie.

Brett added, "Tonight after we meet up to talk about the pranks, we will have a big dinner. I picked a lot of new crops from the farm, and we can have a feast."

"This is going to be a fun day," Poppy said and grinned.

Joe took out a hat and placed slips of paper with their names written on each piece. "Everyone pick a piece of paper and don't tell anybody what name you chose. This is the person you will be pranking."

Poppy put her hand in the hat and was ecstatic when she pulled out Brett's name. She had prepared the ultimate practical joke, and it was only going to work if she chose a person who had a house in Meadow Mews. She was going to empty all of the chests in their house and fill them with apples. Of course she would return all of the items in the chests once the competition was over, but she couldn't wait to see the look on Brett's face when he looked for his emeralds but found a chest full of apples. Poppy wondered if Joe would think her joke was the best one in the competition. She giggled when she thought about her prank. She wondered who was chosen to prank her. The fact that she could be pranked at any moment while she was pranking someone else added to the thrill of the competition.

Brett was the last one to choose a name from the hat. He chose Joe. He wasn't sure which prank he would try on Joe. Brett was upset he had Joe's name because he knew how much Joe disliked being pranked. He reassured himself that Joe had willingly put his name in the hat and he knew he would be pranked. Brett thought of the best prank to play on Joe. Joe had mentioned earlier that he was going to work on the farm. Brett thought of drinking a potion of invisibility and removing wheat from the farm as Joe tended to the land.

As everyone looked at the names they had chosen from the hat, Joe called out, "Let the competition begin!"

2

RAIN CHECK

The gang opened Poppy's door and rushed outside to begin their day of pranking. As they sprinted onto the grassy path, Joe felt a splash of water land on his arm. A light flashed in the distance, and the sound of thunder boomed.

"Oh no!" Poppy cried. "It's raining."

"Is this somebody's idea of a prank?" Helen asked. Her long red hair was drenched with rain.

"I didn't pull this prank," said Nancy.

"Me neither," Callie and Laura said in unison.

A stinging sensation radiated down Brett's arm, and he shrieked in pain, "Ouch!" He pulled his diamond armor from his inventory and put it on. Clutching his enchanted diamond sword, he searched for a skeleton he assumed had shot an arrow into his arm, but he couldn't find one.

Callie cried out, "Someone shot me with an arrow."

"We have to suit up. We need our armor," said

7

Brett, "and then we have to find out who is shooting these arrows."

A barrage of arrows flew across the rainy skies toward the gang. Callie was putting on her armor when an arrow struck her leg. She wailed, "Who is shooting these arrows?" She looked around, but there was no one in sight.

There was a bright flash. Thunder followed. A bolt of lightning shot dangerously close to the wet grassy path near them. The lightning bolt nearly hit Brett. He looked at his arm, inspecting it for burns.

"Are you okay?" asked Callie.

"Yes," Brett replied. "It was just scary."

"I feel like someone is pranking us," said Poppy. "This storm is too intense and unnatural."

"Storms happen all the time," said Callie. "It should pass soon."

Another group of arrows flew toward the gang. Two arrows struck Callie and Poppy, and they shared a bottle of potion as they worked to heal themselves from this surprise attack.

Callie rushed in the direction of the arrows. She thought she saw someone hiding behind a tree and raced toward it. The rainwater made the ground slippery, and she could barely keep her balance. As she reached the tree, Callie saw someone in a blue sweatshirt, but as she approached, the person splashed on a potion of invisibility and disappeared.

"There was someone there!" Callie cried out. Her friends raced to her side.

"Who?" asked Poppy.

Before Callie could reply, two skeletons appeared and unleashed a bunch of arrows at the gang, weakening all of them. Brett was the first one to leap at the skeletons, striking one of the bony beasts with his diamond sword. The bones clanged as he battled the skeleton. Joe attacked the second skeleton. With a few hits from their swords, the skeletons were defeated, but there was no time to celebrate the skeletons' demise, because two new skeletons spawned in their place.

Laura and Callie were in the middle of battling the new skeletons when Poppy hollered, "Look!" Her finger shook as she pointed to a zombie army that lunged toward them. The smell was overpowering. Brett wanted to hold his breath, but he knew it was pointless. You couldn't hold your breath that long, and he needed his energy to battle these undead beasts that walked into Meadow Mews with their arms outstretched.

Poppy raced toward the zombies. As she swung her sword at the closest zombie, Brett stood beside her, splashing potions on the zombies that crowded outside of Poppy's house. One of the zombies ripped her door from the hinges. "My house!" she cried as she slammed her sword into the belly of a zombie. She watched its oozing flesh fall out the gaping hole. She hit the zombie a second time, destroying the beast and quickly picking up the rotten flesh it dropped on the ground.

She raced toward her house, ready to attack the zombie that was destroying the home she had worked so hard to construct. The zombie that ripped her door from the hinges was in the middle of the living room. Poppy hit the zombie with her sword, pulled a potion from her inventory, and doused the zombie until it had one heart left. She plunged her sword into the zombie's flesh and destroyed it. She looked at her door, which was on the wet ground. Poppy wanted to fix the door, but she knew this wasn't the right time because she had to help her friends battle the zombies.

While racing out of her house, she didn't hear a silent creeper trailing her. Brett tried to warn her, but it was too late. By the time Poppy turned around, the explosive enemy destroyed her, and she spawned in her bedroom. When she got up from her bed, she was surprised to see the sun shining.

Callie and Laura put Poppy's door back on its hinges. "Thanks," Poppy said as she took a bite from an apple. She was exhausted from the battle and needed to restore her energy.

Brett, Nancy, Helen, and Joe walked into Poppy's living room and assessed the damage.

"It's not bad," said Brett.

"I agree." Joe surveyed the area. "It could have been a lot worse."

"That was some crazy storm," said Poppy.

"I know," said Laura. "It was so unexpected."

Callie surprised everyone when she announced, "I think it wasn't unexpected. I believe it was a planned attack."

"What are you talking about?" questioned Poppy.

Callie told them about the person she had seen. "I

saw someone behind a tree. I think it was a girl with green hair in a ponytail. She had a blue sweatshirt. I tried to get a closer look, but she splashed a potion on herself and disappeared."

"Who would attack us?" asked Brett.

"I don't know, but do you guys know of anybody who fits that description?" asked Callie.

The group stood in silence as they tried to recall meeting someone with a green ponytail and a blue sweatshirt. None of them had seen anybody who looked like the person Callie had described.

"I can't believe how excited I was to play practical jokes on my friends, and now I am not in the mood for the competition." Poppy frowned.

"We can't let this person destroy all of our fun," Brett said. "We have to start the competition now. The sun is out, and we have a few hours before it sets. I want to play our pranks and have a feast tonight. Let's put all this behind us."

Poppy and the others agreed: they had to stick with the original plan. It was time to start pranking.

3
THE BIG PRANK

Poppy splashed a potion of invisibility on herself before she opened the door to Brett's house. She hoped the potion would last long enough as she emptied all the chests in his house and replaced all the items with apples. She carefully put all of the items from Brett's chests in a large chest she had crafted and placed it in his closet. Poppy giggled as she left Brett's house. When she was standing outside his house, she could see Brett lingering around the farm, staring at Joe. She realized Brett must have chosen Joe as the person he should prank.

She stood by and watched as Brett splashed a potion of invisibility on his body. Once he was invisible, he began to pluck wheat from the ground as Joe tended the farm. Joe was confused and annoyed, because he had just placed seeds on the farm and didn't want the wheat removed. Poppy giggled as she watched this exchange. Joe heard her laughing and turned around.

"Poppy?" he called out.

"Yes," she replied and walked toward Joe.

"I assume someone is pranking me. I know you can't be the one behind this." Joe laughed.

"I'm glad you think it's funny too." Poppy wiped the tears from her eyes. "I found it hilarious, but I'm not the one behind this prank."

Joe didn't have to ask who was pranking him because Brett's potion wore off. He laughed as he stood clutching wheat in his hand.

"Brett!" Joe was shocked. "I can't believe you would pick up the wheat. You know how hard we worked on the farm."

"I know, but you should have seen the look on your face. You had no idea what was going on, and it was really funny." Brett laughed and added, "I only picked a small amount of wheat, and I will reseed the area."

"You're right; it was funny," said Joe.

"It was funny from where I was standing," declared Poppy.

"Will I win the best prank?" questioned Brett.

"We have to see what everyone else has done," replied Joe.

"Who did you prank, Poppy?" asked Brett.

"I'm not going to tell you." She smiled. "You'll find out when everyone else learns about it at the feast."

"I can't wait to hear about everyone's pranks," said Brett.

"Me too," said Poppy.

Brett looked up at the sky. "It's getting dark. I assume most of the people have finished their pranks. It looks like nobody pranked me."

"You're lucky," said Joe.

Brett excused himself. "I just have to go home before the feast. I have to get a few things. I will meet you guys at Poppy's house."

Poppy wanted to ask Brett if she could follow him home. She wanted to be there to see him search through his chests filled with apples. Instead, Poppy watched from afar as Brett entered his house, and once he closed his door, she hurried to a spot outside his home. Joe called out to Poppy, asking her where she was going, but she didn't turn around and respond. She didn't want Joe knowing that she was going to spy through Brett's window.

Poppy reached his house and peeked through Brett's bedroom window. She could see him searching through a chest and pulling out an apple. Poppy almost fell down when Brett stood up and looked out the window and pointed at Poppy. She raced to his door and opened it.

Brett stood in his living room. "I knew it was you!"

"Did you think it was funny?" she asked as she pulled the chest from the closet. "This is where I placed all of your belongings."

"Now that I have my stuff back, I think it's really funny," and then he asked, "Do I get to keep the apples?"

"Of course," Poppy said.

"We should go back to your house and see what the other folks have pulled on each other."

Poppy agreed, and they both headed back to her house. When they arrived there, they found everyone in the living room. Everybody was talking about what pranks they pulled or were pulled on them.

Callie laughed as she explained the prank Laura had pulled on her. "I was running, and I kept falling into a hole every few seconds. I had no idea what was happening to the ground."

"I dug small holes in the ground," said Laura.

Poppy said, "That prank sounds slightly mean."

"It was funny." Laura clarified, "The holes were very small."

"It was funny," said Callie.

"But it wasn't as funny as the prank I pulled on you," said Laura.

"Yes, you did pull a funny one." Callie giggled.

"What did you do?" asked Poppy.

"I TPed Callie to the cold biome." Laura smiled.

"It was really cold," said Callie, "and I didn't have a jacket on hand, but she TPed me back after ten minutes."

"That prank also seems slightly mean," Poppy commented.

Then Nancy told everyone how she and Helen had pranked each other. Helen had sealed Nancy's door shut, and Nancy had filled Helen's living room with chickens. Helen admitted, "Seeing the chickens was funny, but removing them was another story entirely."

Poppy looked around for Joe. "Where's Joe? We need him to judge the contest. We need to figure out who is the winner."

The sky was growing darker, and they questioned if they should go find Joe. Nancy was worried they'd be caught in the middle of another battle with hostile mobs. She explained that she was still recovering from the morning battle in the rain.

"We can't let Joe miss the feast," said Brett. "Also, I'm worried that he isn't here. This isn't like him at all. He is very prompt."

"Maybe he is still being pranked," suggested Callie.

"I was the one chosen to prank Joe, and it happened a while ago. I was invisible and removed wheat while Joe was farming," explained Brett.

"I bet that was very funny," said Laura.

"It was." Poppy told them how she happened to be near the farm when she saw the prank in action. "I wonder if Joe will award it the best prank of the day."

"We don't know what he will choose unless we find him." Brett's voice shook. He was nervous. Being late was out of character for Joe, and Brett wanted to find his friend.

"We should go to his house," said Poppy.

The gang pulled out their armor. The night had settled in, and traveling made them vulnerable to hostile mob attacks. Although Joe lived only down the path from Brett's house, they could still encounter a dangerous and lethal mob. The gang held their diamond swords as they charged toward Joe's house. Brett was the first one to open the door and call out for Joe, but there was no answer.

"Where can he be?" asked Brett.

Poppy and the others stood by Joe's couch. They stared at a hole in the middle of the couch.

"Oh no!" cried Brett. "That looks like a portal!"

"Should we jump in?" asked Poppy.

4
IN THE LIVING ROOM

The crater was large, and Brett could feel the cold air emanating from the opening. He looked down at the massive hole in the couch and said, "We have to jump in."

"What?" Callie's voice cracked.

"I've fallen down two portals before. One brought me to the past, and one to the future. I know Joe is stuck in another time period, and we have to help him," explained Brett.

"But what happens if we get trapped in that time period?" Laura questioned. "How will we get out?"

"I agree," said Callie. "I'm not taking the plunge. It's too scary."

"Joe is a good friend, and I'm going," Brett announced. "You don't have to come with me." Brett hopped in the portal. He didn't look back to see who had followed him on this journey. As he fell deeper into the portal, he felt goose bumps on his arms. The cold air was even more frigid than the past two portals, and he felt as if he were turning into an icicle. With only his light blue T-shirt to keep him warm, Brett was freezing. He hugged himself to keep warm, but it didn't help. There was nothing he could do to warm up. The deeper he traveled, the colder it became. After a couple of minutes, Brett wondered if he'd survive. He hoped he didn't freeze on the trip through the portal. He wanted to land in whatever biome or time period Joe had been thrown into, and he wanted to help Joe escape.

Brett heard a sound coming from above him. He looked up and saw a pair of black boots. It was Poppy. She had followed right behind him. Although he was freezing, his heart warmed with the thought of Poppy helping him find Joe. Knowing Poppy was there made Brett a bit less scared. Before he had time to call out to Poppy, he landed on the ground with a loud thump. Sand shot up from the ground and got into his eyes. The sand stung his eyes, and he began to cry.

"Brett," Poppy hollered as she landed on the ground next to him. She brushed the sand from her eyes and questioned, "Is it always that cold in the portal?"

"Yes."

"You should have warned us. We could have put on jackets. I'm only wearing this jumpsuit. I was freezing," Poppy said as she jumped in place to help warm up her body.

"Us?" asked Brett.

"Yes," Poppy said. "The others agreed to jump in, too."

"Really? Where are they?"

"They'll be here soon unless they backed out." Poppy looked up at the sky she had fallen out of. There was no visible sign of the portal, and Poppy wondered if their friends had joined them.

"I hope so." Brett stared at the sky as he spoke.

The sky was getting dark, and Poppy was worried they'd be vulnerable to a hostile mob attack. "If they don't show up soon, I should start crafting a house. I don't want us to be out all night. It's not safe."

Brett looked around the landscape. All he could see was sand. There was nothing but a large stretch of sand and a few dunes. "I wonder where we are. I can't figure out what time period we are in. Can you?"

Poppy wasn't paying attention to Brett. She was too busy searching through her inventory to find the items needed to construct a house for them. "What did you say?"

"I said I wonder what time period we are in," Brett repeated.

"I have no idea. It just looks like your standard desert to me," said Poppy.

"I just want to do a quick exploration to see if we find any clues."

"Now?" Poppy questioned as she pulled wooden planks from her inventory. "We have to build a house to sleep in. I think we should construct it here in case any of our friends show up. We will be right where the portal drops people."

"That's a good idea. We can find out what time period we are in when we wake up in the morning. Do you need any help with the house?"

Poppy handed a wooden plank to Brett and told him what he needed to do in order to help her finish the house before sunset. They worked tirelessly, and when the sun had finally set, they were placing the final window on the house. Brett pulled out a torch and placed it on the side of the house.

When they closed the door, they quickly crafted beds in the small, one-room home. Brett could barely keep his eyes open as he crawled into the bed. He closed his eyes but opened them when he heard Poppy say, "I can't believe our friends didn't go through the portal."

"It was a lot to ask of someone. They had no idea if they would ever get back home. It's a scary endeavor."

"I know, but they seemed fine with the idea. They all said they would jump in right after me. I can't believe they lied to me." Poppy was upset.

"I don't think they lied to you. I bet they wanted to jump into the portal, but they got scared and backed out," Brett reasoned.

"I guess you're right," said Poppy.

"We have to get some sleep. Tomorrow we need to do a thorough search of the desert. We have to find Joe," said Brett.

"I hope we find him," Poppy said as she closed her eyes.

The two friends were drifting off to sleep when they heard a knock at the door.

5

BACK IN HISTORY

"Who's there?" asked Poppy.

Brett walked to the door and opened it. He smiled when he saw Nancy, Helen, Callie, and Laura standing in the doorway.

"We are so glad this was your house," said Nancy.

"I knew Poppy designed it," Callie remarked. "She has a certain signature style. I always know when she has built something."

"Can we fit in here?" asked Helen.

"Of course," Brett replied, but as they crowded into the tiny living room, he wasn't certain they could fit in the house. They were standing so close to each other, they barely had room to breathe.

"I can expand the house," Poppy said with a yawn. "I'll take a few things from my inventory and build an extension."

"It's not safe. We can't go outside," explained Nancy. "We just battled skeletons and a witch."

"A witch?" questioned Brett. "In the desert?"

"The swamp borders the desert," replied Callie.

"Where did you land when you were dropped from the portal?" asked Brett.

Callie explained how they were dropped on the edge of the desert by the swamp. It was dusk, and they were forced to battle a series of hostile mobs. They were ready to give up when they found this small house.

"When we saw this house, we knew we had found you guys. We've had such an awful experience ever since we landed in this time period," said Laura. Then she asked, "Do you know what time period we are in?"

"We don't know," said Brett.

"I guess you haven't found Joe?" asked Nancy.

"No, we also have to do that in the morning," replied Brett.

Poppy surveyed the room and announced, "I think it will be very tight, but I believe we can all sleep in the house. I'll help you guys craft beds."

The gang worked together to craft beds, and after a good night's sleep, everyone was ready to find Joe and figure out what time period they were in. Callie was the first one out of the house. The sun was shining, and she breathed in the dry, hot air. "I forgot how hot it is in the desert," Callie said as she tried to block the sun's rays with her hands.

Laura squinted. "I'm already sweating. Today is going to be very hot."

Helen sprinted from the house and hollered, "Watch out!"

A sand-colored mob lumbered toward Callie and Laura. It almost appeared camouflaged in the desert landscape, but on closer inspection they saw that it looked similar to a zombie. Laura looked up and shrieked, "What's that?"

Callie's voice shook. "It's a husk."

The husk's arms were extended, and the beast grabbed Callie. She tried to pull away, but it was too late. She had been attacked. Once the desert mob touched Callie, she was struck with an incredible hunger. She wanted to eat every item in her inventory. Her stomach growled, and the only word she could speak was "Apple."

Laura swung her diamond sword at the husk's belly and destroyed the beast, which dropped a small piece of rotten flesh. Laura pulled an apple from her inventory and handed it to Callie. Callie finished the apple in one bite.

"I've never been that hungry in my life," confessed Callie.

"When husks attack, they leave you with an intense hunger," explained Nancy. "I've only encountered a husk once before, and it hit me. I wound up eating everything I had, and I was still hungry."

Brett and Poppy stood in the doorway with their mouths gaping as they watched an army of husks charge toward them.

"I don't understand how hostile mobs can form. It's daylight," said Poppy.

"Husks can spawn anytime. The sun doesn't bother them," said Callie. "They are creatures of the desert."

"This is going to be a real challenge," said Brett as he put on his armor and grabbed his enchanted diamond sword and raced toward the husks that were ready to attack them. He slammed his sword into two husks. The beasts were destroyed and dropped rotten flesh.

The battle lasted longer than they expected, and they were all exhausted and hungry. The gang ate everything in their inventories. Callie remarked, "We have to restock our food supplies."

"Yes," said Helen. "There is no way we will survive unless we find some food."

Poppy sighed. "Food is so hard to find in the desert."

"If we can find a lake, we can fish," said Nancy. "I have a fishing rod."

"Great idea," exclaimed Poppy.

As they walked through the desert and searched for a lake, Brett wanted to suggest that he build a farm. However, he remembered he had once created a farm in the desert, but it wasn't an easy task, and he knew that it would be days before they'd be able to see anything grow. Instead he suggested they try to find someone who might be willing to trade supplies for food. "I have a lot of emeralds," he remarked. "Maybe we can trade those."

"That's a good idea," said Callie. "It doesn't look like we are going to stumble upon a lake anytime soon. All I can see is sand."

The gang was thirsty and hot as they made their way through the cacti-filled desert.

"I feel like we've landed in the past," said Callie.

"What makes you think that?" questioned Nancy.

"I don't believe anything has been created yet. I feel like we have been walking forever, and we haven't seen one desert temple or another person. If we don't find someone, we will all be destroyed. We need food," remarked Callie.

"I see something!" Poppy called out.

The gang followed Poppy as she hurried toward a small hut in the distance. When she reached the hut, she called out, "Hello. Is anybody home?"

A small man wearing a green cap opened the door. "Yes," he said. "Who are you?"

"We are lost," said Poppy, "What town is this?"

"Sandy Vista," replied the man.

"What?" Callie put her hand over her mouth. "It can't be."

"It is," he said.

"But Sandy Vista doesn't really exist," Callie replied.

"Of course it does. I live here," he laughed.

Brett added, "Sandy Vista was a place of legends. It's a lost city. People always talk about it, but nobody has ever been there. People have spent their lifetimes traveling around the Overworld searching for Sandy Vista, but nobody has ever found it."

"It appears that you guys have found it," the man said with a smile. "I'm Jacques."

The gang introduced themselves and asked Jacques

if he had any food. "I do, but I can also show you a great place to find food. Just follow me."

The gang trailed behind Jacques as he led them through miles of undeveloped desert. Their stomachs let out a collective grumble, and they hoped he'd lead them to food soon.

6

SANDY VISTA

I t felt as if they had been walking for hours. The sun beat down on them, and the gang was losing their energy. Brett asked, "Where is the food?"

"You must be patient," replied Jacques. "Things haven't been very easy for us lately."

"What is happening?" questioned Poppy.

Jacques stopped and pulled a bunch of apples and bottles of milk from his inventory. "Take these. I see you guys are starving and thirsty, and these will help you regain your energy. This journey might be longer than expected."

The gang thanked Jacques as they gulped the milk and finished the apples.

Jacques asked, "Do you guys feel better?"

The color had been restored to their cheeks, and they all agreed they felt better. Nancy asked, "What is going on in Sandy Vista?"

Jacques's eyes filled with tears. "There is a villain that is terrorizing us. She wants to destroy our beautiful town."

"How?" asked Nancy.

"This person has decided to spend all of her time trying to ruin the town. She has magic abilities, which are tough to battle," explained Jacques.

"Like what?" asked Brett.

"She is able to pour a potion on her body, and then she disappears."

Brett said, "That's not magic. She has a potion of invisibility."

"What's that?" questioned Jacques.

"Have you never brewed a potion before?" Poppy was shocked, but then she remembered they were far back in the past in a town that survived only in legends. Sandy Vista didn't even make it into history books because nobody was certain the town had ever existed. Poppy hoped they could help Sandy Vista survive. She knew that would change the shape of history, but she didn't care. She wanted to save it so people could visit the miles of unspoiled stretches of desert. The landscape was stunning.

Jacques confessed that he had never brewed a potion. "I'd love to learn how to brew one."

"When we get back to your house, I will help you craft a brewing stand and teach you all of the essential steps to brewing," said Brett.

"That would be incredible," said Jacques as he continued walking, and the group saw a large desert temple in the distance. Jacques said, "That's where we will find food. We have a king—"

Before he could continue, Poppy interrupted. "King Jed and Queen Gail," Poppy spit out their names.

"Yes, how do you know them?" asked Jacques.

"We all know them. They are legends. They were the rulers of the lost city," Poppy explained.

"Why is Sandy Vista a lost city? You guys are here now. How can it be considered lost?" Jacques was confused.

Brett took a deep breath and exhaled, then said, "I know this is going to sound a little farfetched, but we are from the future."

"The future? What do you mean?"

Brett told Jacques about the portal and his other time travels, and then Poppy added, "We all grew up hearing about Sandy Vista. I always wanted to go there. It sounded beautiful. Now that I am here, I see that it is even more stunning in real life. I am so glad I'm here."

Jacques eyebrows creased, and he looked tense. "What is going to happen to Sandy Vista? Can you help us? I don't want Sandy Vista to become a lost city."

"Neither do we," said Nancy. "We will help you keep the town in existence. Perhaps that's why we were brought back to this time period."

Brett wanted to remind Nancy that the reason they were back in time was because of Joe. He wanted to find his friend. Brett hoped Joe had also found the desert temple and was with the king and queen. In the folktales about King Jed and Queen Gail, they were always known to be compassionate and fair rulers. As the crew reached the temple, a man in an orange robe sprinted toward them.

"Colin," Jacques called out.

"The king and queen are missing." Colin's voice cracked.

"What?" Jacques hollered.

"They are missing. I worry that something serious has happened to them," said Colin.

"We will find them," Jacques said. "These people will help us," he said as he pointed to the gang.

"Who are these people?" asked Colin. "Can we trust them?"

"You can trust us," Brett spoke for the group.

"Why?" questioned Colin.

Poppy said, "We want to help your town. We think it's a special place."

Colin said, "You're going to have to earn my trust."

"Do you have any suspects?" asked Brett. "Any idea who would capture the king and queen?"

"At first I thought the woman with the green hair was behind it. She has been terrorizing our town. But I found someone lurking around the temple, and I decided to take him as a prisoner. I don't trust him," said Colin.

"Can we meet the suspect?" asked Jacques.

"Yes," Colin replied. "I'll lead you to the person."

The group entered the temple. It was much cooler inside the temple than it was outside. The gang was happy to escape the strong sun and the heat and to walk through the cool temple's spacious living room. They looked over at the empty thrones. Colin said, "That is where you'd normally find King Jed and Queen Gail."

Colin led them downstairs into a dark, musty basement. Another man in a tan robe was standing guard in front of a small cell. The gang gasped when they saw the person who stood behind the bars.

7

BREWING LESSONS

"Joe." Brett grabbed the bars and tried to open the gate.

"Stand back," said Colin. "Don't touch the bars."

Joe was filthy and famished. "Please, these are my friends."

"Are you working together? We have to capture all of them," Colin said.

Jacques said, "These people aren't our enemy. They told me they would teach me how to brew potions."

"Potions?" questioned Colin. "Nobody can brew them. They're magic."

"No," explained Brett. "I can teach you guys how to brew, and then you can craft potions that make you invisible or gain strength or speed or health."

"That can't be. You're fooling us," said Colin.

"Colin," Jacques said, "they're telling the truth."

"Prove it," said Colin.

"I just need a brewing stand," said Brett. "Mine is in my house."

"Very convenient," remarked Colin. "Why don't you go home and get it?"

"They can't go home," said Jacques. "They're from the future."

"Okay, I've heard enough. This is crazy. Nobody can travel through time," said Colin.

Callie pulled a brewing stand from her inventory. "I brought one because we were traveling, and I knew I might need one for the practical joke competition."

"Practical joke competition?" questioned Colin. "What is that?"

Poppy started to explain the rules of the competition and list all of the practical jokes she had played, but Callie interrupted her. "This isn't the time. We have to teach these people how to make potions. They need to learn how to defend themselves from this enemy."

"Yes," said Jacques. "Please teach us how to brew potions."

"I will," said Callie, "but not until you let my friend Joe out of your makeshift jail. He doesn't deserve to be there."

Jacques said, "Okay." He walked toward the jail cell, but Colin stopped him.

"Are you sure we should trust these people?" asked Colin.

"What do I have to do to convince you?" Jacques was annoyed. "We have to trust them. They are our only hope."

"Our only hope?" asked Colin. "Can that be true?"

Callie pulled a bottle and a fermented spider eye from her inventory. "Do you want to learn how to become invisible?"

Colin paused and looked over at Joe. "Okay, I do." Colin opened the gate and let Joe free.

"Are you okay?" Brett rushed to his friend's side.

"I am now." Joe smiled.

Callie called Brett over to the potion stand. "Brett, can you help me teach these guys how to brew?"

"Of course," said Brett as he stood by the brewing stand. As Callie started to teach Jacques and Colin about the potions, a thunderous noise roared from the outside.

"What's that?" cried Colin.

"It sounds like we're under attack again." Jacques rushed outside and hollered, "An Ender Dragon. The villain spawned the Ender Dragon."

The gang put on their armor and grabbed their bows and arrows as they hurried outside to battle the lethal dragon. The Ender Dragon flew toward the gang, and they unleashed a barrage of arrows that struck the belly of the beast. The dragon roared as it lost a heart. The dragon swooped down at the group, nearly hitting Callie. She regained her footing and pulled a potion from her inventory and splashed it on the beast that flew next to her.

The dragon lost another heart. Colin watched in awe as the gang used arrows and potions to destroy the beast. The Ender Dragon was weakened, and bits of light shone from its muscular body. The dragon's health deteriorated until it exploded. Colin covered his ears as he watched the powerful dragon explode, and his eyes widened as an egg was dropped and a portal to the End spawned in the center of Sandy Vista.

Colin walked over to the portal. Callie screamed, "Don't go too close. You don't want to go to the End."

"What's the End?" asked Colin.

"It's a place where the Ender Dragon resides. It's very dark, but if you destroy the Ender Dragon in the End, you can go to the End city, where you can find many treasures," explained Brett. "But this isn't the time to travel there. We have to help you guys battle this enemy."

Nancy said, "Jacques, you had mentioned there was a villain. Who is she?"

"I don't know her name, but she has green hair," said Jacques.

Callie interrupted, "Does she wear a blue sweatshirt?"

"Yes," exclaimed Jacques. "Do you know her?"

"I saw her," Callie said, "when we were back in Meadow Mews."

"Where is that?" asked Colin.

"It's the town we live in, but I don't think it exists yet," explained Callie, "which makes me realize that this villain is able to travel through time."

"She must be extremely powerful," remarked Jacques.

"Yes," said Callie, "but we will defeat her. We will save Sandy Vista."

"But that will change the course of history. Isn't that bad?" questioned Brett. "Aren't we supposed to let things stay the way they are? I mean, I also want Sandy Vista to survive, but we have to be true to the history of the Overworld."

"I think we were sent back in time to change the future. We are here to rewrite history," said Joe.

Callie added, "Since that villain was also in Meadow Mews, I believe she must be focusing on destroying our town too. This means that if we defeat her in the past, we won't have to deal with her in the future."

Brett said, "That makes sense. This villain is a time traveler. So if we stop her here, we can save both towns."

"Please save our town," said Colin.

"Can we go back into the temple and have you teach us how to brew potions?" asked Jacques.

The gang walked back into the temple, and Callie stood in front of the brewing stand teaching everyone how to make potions. When she finished her first batch of the potion of invisibility, she poured it on Colin, and they watched as he disappeared.

8

SAVE THE QUEEN

"That was awesome!" said Colin. "I was invisible. Teach me how to brew other potions."

Callie looked through her inventory. "I don't have too many ingredients on me. What about you guys?" she asked her friends.

"My inventory is almost empty," Brett reminded her. "We also don't have food. Jacques, you had promised us some food."

"Yes, we have a farm here, so you can refill your inventories with food. Also, there is a large lake that is filled with fish. I can lead you there now," said Jacques.

"Not so fast," said Colin.

"What?" Jacques was confused.

"I think we should negotiate a trade. If we give them access to our food, they will teach us how to source ingredients to craft potions," suggested Jacques.

"Of course we will agree to that. We don't need to

negotiate a formal trade. That's just what friends do for each other. They help each other out," explained Poppy.

Brett said, "Before we teach you how to source the ingredients, we must warn you that we have to travel to the Nether."

"The Nether? Really?" Jacques's voice shook. "I've only heard about the Nether but have never traveled there. It sounds very scary."

"If you stick with us," said Poppy, "it won't be bad. There aren't many people who enjoy being in the Nether, but it's a great place to gather ingredients for potions. We can get netherrack and Nether wart and ghast tears and other valuable resources in the Nether. Since you guys live in the desert, you have the advantage of being acclimated to the heat. The Nether is very hot, which is always hard for me," confessed Poppy.

"How do we get there?" asked Jacques.

"We will build a portal," replied Brett. "I have all the supplies we need to craft a portal to the Nether."

Brett walked outside of the temple, and the gang followed him. As Brett pulled obsidian from his inventory, a voice cried for help in the distance.

"Who is that?" asked Poppy.

"Help!" the voice cried out again.

"Oh my!" said Colin. "That sounds like Queen Gail."

"It does!" Jacques exclaimed. "We have to help her!"

"Help!" the voice cried and grew fainter.

Brett raced toward the sound of the distressed voice. "It sounds like it's coming from this direction."

The gang dashed toward the voice, which called out again. The voice was clearer and louder, and they were hopeful they would find her.

"Queen Gail!" Colin called out. "Where are you? We are here to help you."

Poppy's braids bounced as she hurried toward the sound of the queen. She was the first to see Queen Gail's crown. She hollered, "She's over here. Right by the swamp."

Queen Gail was standing on the edge of the murky water, and a woman with green hair held a sword toward her back.

"Leave her alone," Jacques hollered at the villain.

She laughed. "Why should I?"

"Who are you?" Callie sprinted toward the villain, and she splashed a potion of harming on the green-haired trickster.

"You don't need to know who I am," the villain cried out as she lost a heart. "You just need to know that I'm here to destroy you." The villain pulled a potion of healing from her inventory and took a quick gulp. "You are never going to stop me."

As the villain lunged at Callie, Queen Gail used the energy from her remaining heart to slam her sword into the green-haired woman, but the villain splashed a potion of invisibility on herself and vanished.

"Her name is Veronica," explained the queen as she pulled milk from her inventory and took a sip to regain her energy. "And who are you guys?"

"They are helping us save Sandy Vista," explained Jacques.

"Good, you've recruited an army," Queen Gail said as she readjusted her crown. Despite her traumatic capture, her curly red hair was flawless and her pink gown shimmered.

"Army?" Nancy questioned. "I don't think we're an army. We are just people who want to help you."

"Call yourself whatever you like. We just need you to help us. As you might already know, Veronica has captured King Jed. We have to get him," said the queen.

"Where is he?" asked Colin.

"She kept us trapped in a mine right out of the desert. I think I know the way," said the queen.

The sky grew darker, and a full moon rose above the swampy biome. Two bats flew close to the group's heads, and everyone worried they would be attacked by hostile mobs.

Poppy suggested, "Do you think we should build a shelter? It's getting dark, and the swamp has many hostile mobs."

"We can't waste time," said the queen. "We have to find King Jed. He is trapped in a mine, and I can't sleep knowing that he is there."

Poppy understood this reasoning, but she also knew that they were going to be incredibly vulnerable to hostile mobs. As they followed the queen toward the mine, they could hear a bouncing noise growing louder.

"It sounds like slimes," remarked Helen.

Boing! Boing! Boing! . . .

Poppy slammed her sword into the slime, and it broke into smaller pieces. The gang used their weapons to destroy the slimy swamp mobs. When the final slime was destroyed, they continued on until they heard a shrill laugh.

"Oh no!" Poppy cried. "It's a witch."

Poppy had a slight fear of witches, and her body tensed. She took a deep breath as she pulled a potion from her inventory, readying herself for an attack.

As the purple-robed witch lunged toward them, her laugh grew louder. She splashed a potion on the queen, leaving the queen exhausted and unable to move as she stood by the witch's house.

Brett and Poppy raced to the witch. Poppy splashed a potion on the witch, and Brett pierced the witch with his sword. The witch was able to splash a potion at Brett, and he stood next to the queen. Both Brett and the queen were motionless and felt a wave of exhaustion.

"We have to help them," said Helen, and she handed the two a potion of healing.

Poppy was surprised when she destroyed the witch using her potions and enchanted diamond sword.

As the queen regained her strength, she said, "Maybe you guys were right. Maybe this trip is too dangerous."

"No," said Poppy. "You were right. We have to save the king."

9
NIGHT ATTACK

The night grew darker, and they pulled torches from their inventories to light the path. Then they heard a shrill laugh again.

"Another witch!" cried Poppy.

"We have to get out of the swamp," said Brett.

"I think we should build a house," said the queen. "This is just going to get worse."

"You're in luck," said Brett. "Poppy, Callie, and Laura are expert builders. In our time period, they might be the most famous builders in the Overworld."

Poppy blushed, but it was dark out, and nobody saw she was embarrassed. "I will build anything if I don't have to battle another witch."

"We will destroy the witch," said Queen Gail. "Just build the house."

The gang charged toward the witch as Callie, Laura, and Poppy pulled everything from their inventories and began to craft a house faster than they had ever built anything. Callie placed wooden planks on the swampy ground, and Laura helped build the foundation. Poppy placed a window and the door to finish the house in record time. Poppy walked in and began crafting beds. She said, "This is going to be very tight, but it's better than nothing."

When the final bed was finished, Callie said, "We have to find the others."

Callie, Laura, and Poppy set out to find the rest of the group, but they were nowhere in sight. "I thought the witch was right near us," said Laura.

"Do you think somebody captured them?" asked Poppy.

"Or the witch destroyed them?" questioned Callie.

Laura didn't think one witch could destroy that many people. "The witch was outnumbered. Veronica has to be behind this."

They heard a witch's laugh in the distance, and Callie said, "We should go back to the house. We will search for them in the morning when it's safer."

Poppy wanted to continue to search for Brett and the others. "These are my best friends. I can't stop looking for them."

"The queen felt the same way, but even she realized that staying out after dark is way too dangerous. We need to stay in the house and search in the morning. If we are destroyed, there will be nobody left to save the king and find our friends," Callie reasoned with Poppy.

Poppy understood and reluctantly went to the

house and crawled into bed. Within seconds, she was fast asleep. She dreamed she was in Meadow Mews building a tree house. She was crafting the ladder to the tree house when she woke up and realized she was still in the past and Brett was still missing. Her heart sank.

Callie was putting on her armor. "We have to get going. The sun has just come out, and we need as much time as we can get."

Laura was also placing her armor on and said, "Yes, we have to find the mine. I'm sure everybody is trapped there."

"How are we going to find this mine without Queen Gail?" asked Poppy.

"I don't know, but we are going to search every hole and crevice until we find it," said Callie.

The gang sprinted from the house in search of the mine. The swamp biome was larger than they expected, and when they finally reached the hilly biome, they were tired.

"I don't have any food in my inventory," said Callie.

"None of us does," said Poppy. "We are going to have to conserve our energy."

"That's easier said than done," said Laura.

The trio felt like they were walking forever as they searched for the mine, which seemed to be nonexistent. They were ready to give up when they heard a familiar voice in the distance.

"Poppy!" the voice called out.

"Brett!" Poppy rushed toward her friend.

Brett was leading the pack, as the other friends were behind him. "We're here," he said breathlessly.

"What happened to you guys?" asked Callie.

"We looked for you, but it was as if you had disappeared," remarked Laura.

Nancy explained, "We were trapped in the witch's house. Once we destroyed her, Veronica showed up and splashed a potion of weakness on all of us. We each had one heart left, and she forced us to enter the witch's house. When the morning came, we ganged up on her and destroyed her."

"She is going to want revenge," said Queen Gail.

"We are going to have to battle her again. We can do it," said Helen.

Callie admitted that she was worried they were too weak to battle. "We each have only one heart left. We have no food in our inventories."

Colin, Jacques, and Queen Gail gave everyone food, and once the gang feasted, they followed Queen Gail to the mine.

"I know it's right here," she said as she walked through a path thick with leaves. "There has to be an entrance over here."

"I think I see it!" Brett called out.

Everyone rushed over to Brett as he pulled out a torch and entered the dimly lit mine in search of King Jed. As they stepped inside, Queen Gail said, "Yes, this is the place. Veronica is holding him in the prison in the stronghold."

They followed Queen Gail down a dark path that

led to a door. She opened it and screamed. Veronica was on the other side of the door and splashed a potion of harming on the queen, leaving her with one heart.

Brett lunged toward Veronica and slammed his diamond sword into her unarmored arm, weakening her. Poppy rushed to Brett's side, splashed a potion on Veronica, and called out, "We are here to save King Jed. You have to stop terrorizing Sandy Vista."

"And Meadow Mews," said Callie.

"Never!" Veronica smiled.

Brett continued to battle Veronica, making room for the others to dash down the stairs into the stronghold and save King Jed. Poppy was the only person who stayed with Brett and helped him contain Veronica.

"Why are you doing this?" asked Poppy.

"Because I can," Veronica said as she pierced Poppy's leg with her diamond sword. Poppy cried out in pain.

"We are going to stop you," said Brett as he leaped at Veronica.

Poppy was about to splash a potion on Veronica when she vanished. Poppy said, "She TPed somewhere."

"We have to find out where," said Brett.

The others hurried toward Brett and Poppy. Queen Gail was smiling, and King Jed stood next to her. "We found him!" she exclaimed.

10

NETHER AGAIN

"We have to find Veronica and stop her!" cried Poppy.

"Of course," said the queen, "but we also have to be prepared and have a plan."

The group agreed that they needed to come up with a plan. Colin said, "We still don't know how to brew potions. Can you help us learn?"

"We should go back to the temple, and we will teach you," said Brett, but Poppy reminded him that they were running low on ingredients, and they remembered the trip to the Nether.

"Let's build a portal," said Colin.

"The Nether." Queen Gail paused. "I don't want to go there. I've heard stories about the Nether, and it seems like a horrid place to visit."

King Jed added, "We don't think we'd survive in the Nether. Neither Queen Gail nor I is a solid fighter.

I know there are multiple mobs there that shoot fireballs, and I don't think we'd be able to fight them off."

"Do you want to learn how to craft potions?" asked Brett.

"Yes," King Jed replied.

"Then you have to visit the Nether. We aren't going to travel there and gather ingredients for you. That isn't fair," said Brett.

Nancy said, "I'm a treasure hunter, and Nether fortresses are great places to find treasure, which means I've been to the Nether multiple times. I know it sounds scary, but if you stick with us, we will help you navigate the area."

"You'd do that for us?" asked Queen Gail.

"Yes," said Nancy. "We want to help you and the people of Sandy Vista."

Brett pulled obsidian from his inventory and began to craft a portal. Queen Gail shook as she watched him build it. "I'm very nervous," she confessed.

"Don't worry. We will be by your side the entire time. I will guide you," Nancy said as she led Queen Gail and King Jed onto the portal. They stood close to each other as the purple mist surrounded them and they made their way to the Nether.

Landing in the Nether was easier than Queen Gail had expected. The trip through the portal took mere seconds, and when they arrived, they were next to a lava river and a stunning lava fall was in the distance. The skies were free of hostile mobs. There were two zombie pigmen walking toward them, but Nancy warned that they must not stare at the pigmen.

"If you don't engage, the pigmen will leave you alone," said Nancy.

Helen spotted a Nether fortress in the distance. "We need to go to that fortress. That is where we'll find netherrack."

As the gang traveled to the fortress, two ghasts flew toward them, shooting a barrage of fireballs. Queen Gail gasped, "What do we do?"

"I'll show you," said Nancy. "Just stay beside me."

A fireball flew at Nancy, and Queen Gail marveled as she saw Nancy use her fist to deflect the fireball. The ball shot back at the ghast and destroyed it.

"You're so talented," exclaimed Queen Gail.

"You can do it too," said Nancy.

The second fireball flew toward them, and Nancy said, "You can do it, Queen."

Queen Gail's hand shook as she neared the fireball. Then she struck the ball, and it flew toward the ghast, obliterating it.

"You did it!" exclaimed Nancy.

"I can't believe it," said Queen Gail.

"Pick up the ghast tear," instructed Nancy. "You can use that to brew a potion of regeneration."

Queen Gail picked up the ghast tear and placed it in her inventory. "I can't believe I was able to destroy a ghast."

"Wow," King Jed said, "I'm so impressed."

"There's no time to celebrate Queen Gail's destroying her first ghast," said Joe. "We have to head to the fortress. We must gather as many supplies as we can before we head back to Sandy Vista."

The gang headed toward the fortress, but once they reached the entrance, they were met by a group of blazes that guarded the fortress.

"What's that?" King Jed asked. He pointed to the yellow beasts floating from the ground and into the air as they shot a series of fireballs at the group.

"Blazes!" cried Helen.

"Help me fight them." Queen Gail was confident that she could battle them now that she had destroyed her first ghast.

Nancy pulled snowballs from her inventory and handed one to Queen Gail. "These are great for fighting blazes."

Nancy flung a snowball at the blaze, destroying the beast. A blaze rod dropped to the ground, and Nancy grabbed it. As Queen Gail destroyed the second blaze with Nancy's snowball, Nancy told her, "You need to keep the blaze rod. You can use it to craft a potion."

"Wow," said Queen Gail, "we are certainly getting a lot of ingredients on this trip."

"We are," said Nancy. "Now we have to enter the fortress, and I will help you search for everything you need to brew, but first I have to unearth the treasure."

"The treasure?" Brett was annoyed. "This isn't the time to search for treasure. We have to battle Veronica, and we need all of the supplies we can get here. We don't need to look for treasure."

Nancy shrugged. "Okay, I guess you're right, but if we have any extra time, I will search for the treasure."

Poppy called out, "Soul sand and netherrack." She walked toward the staircase. "We have to pick all of this."

The gang crowded around the staircase as they gathered the soul sand and netherrack, filling up their inventories.

As they picked the final pieces of netherrack, Joe called out in pain. He turned around to find a dark wither skeleton standing inches from the ingredient. The mob slammed its sword against Joe's arm, and he wailed. Brett leaped toward the wither skeleton as he pierced the undead mob of the Nether with his diamond sword. Brett destroyed the mob with one strike and picked up the wither skeleton skull that fell on the floor of the Nether fortress.

"There are probably more of those," remarked Poppy. "We have to be very careful."

"What was that?" questioned Colin.

"It's a wither skeleton," said Poppy, "and there is another one right behind you."

Before the second wither skeleton could attack Colin, Jacques took out his bow and arrow and shot an arrow at the skeleton, obliterating the beast.

"We have enough supplies," said Brett. "We should head back to Sandy Vista and start brewing."

"Good idea," said Jacques.

The gang was ready to exit the Nether fortress when they heard a bouncing sound.

Boing! Boing! Boing!

"What's that sound?" asked Colin. As he questioned the group, the room started to fill with large cubes.

"Those are magma cubes," said Brett as he slammed his sword into a magma cube and it broke into smaller cubes.

"What are those?" questioned Colin.

"It doesn't matter what they are," said Nancy. "Just battle them."

"They are just like slimes," said Poppy, "but they're in the Nether." Poppy destroyed the smaller cubes.

"You have to pick up the magma cream," instructed Brett. "It's vital for many potions."

The gang worked together to battle the magma cubes and pick up the cream it had dropped on the ground. As they finished battling the final magma cube, they heard a sinister laugh.

"I see you guys are working together. How nice!" Veronica stood in the center of the Nether fortress. "What if I told you there is no Sandy Vista to return to? That I destroyed it while you were away on this vacation?"

"Vacation?" King Jed pointed his enchanted diamond sword at Veronica. He lunged toward her, ready to strike, but she vanished.

"Do you think what she said was true?" Colin's voice shook as he spoke those words. "Do you think that she destroyed Sandy Vista? That we don't have a home to return to?"

"I think there's only one way we can find out," said Brett as he raced out of the Nether fortress and stepped onto the portal.

11

HIDING FROM THE HUSKS

lthough the trip back on the portal took seconds, it felt like an eternity. The gang huddled together as they nervously anticipated spawning in a place that might be destroyed.

"I am so scared," confessed Jacques.

"We all are," said King Jed.

When they spawned in Sandy Vista, the gang let out a collective sigh when they saw the temple standing. A robed man approached them.

"Brian," Colin called out, "Sandy Vista is still here?"

"Yes." Brian had a perplexed expression. "Why should it be gone?"

"Veronica," explained Colin. "She told us she destroyed it."

"She's tried. She has created a husk spawner. I was able to deactivate it. It was in the mine. She attempted to trap me down there, but I escaped."

"We have to stop her," said Jacques.

"We do," said Brian, and then he screamed, "Oh no!" as he saw an army of husks enter Sandy Vista. "She built another spawner! We need to find out where it is."

"We have to battle the husks," said Colin.

Poppy stared at the husks. She feared the intense hunger these creatures inflicted upon them. With no food in her inventory, she didn't think she'd be able to survive an attack from these beasts. Poppy wanted to find a portal and make her way back to Meadow Mews. She wished they were still in the middle of judging the practical joke competition and having a feast. She didn't want to start a battle against a powerful enemy.

Brett was the first person to strike a husk. He struck a husk with his diamond sword and destroyed it. He then moved on to a second husk, but it struck him. His stomach began to growl, and his food and health bar diminished. He didn't have any energy to strike another husk. He just wanted to eat. Brett could see the farm behind the temple. He wanted to stop the battle and sprint to the farm and pick an apple, but he didn't have the energy.

Queen Gail stood alongside Brett, battling the husks. She could see Brett's energy diminish, and she handed him a glass of milk. "Quick, drink this."

The milk quenched his thirst and replenished his energy, but he really wanted food. He thanked Queen Gail for the milk and asked if she had a spare apple she could give him. She handed him an apple. "After we defeat these husks, we will have a feast," she promised.

Brett looked at the never-ending army of husks that were in the middle of the sandy desert. He wasn't sure they would ever defeat these beasts. As the gang battled the husks, more spawned, replacing the ones they had destroyed.

"This battle is pointless," said Brian. "We should go to the stronghold and destroy the new spawner. Who wants to go with me?"

Brett volunteered, "I'll go. I want to destroy the spawner."

Joe and Poppy followed behind Brett and Brian as they made their way to the mine to deactivate the spawner. When they arrived at the mine, Veronica was standing at the front of the entrance. She held her diamond sword in one hand and a bottle of potion in the other.

"Where do you think you're going?" she asked with a sinister laugh.

"We are going to deactivate the spawner," Brett said as he slammed his sword into Veronica's shoulder.

She splashed a potion on Brett, weakening him and leaving him with one heart. "I don't think so."

"It's just one of you and four of us," said Poppy, and she leaped at Veronica.

Veronica splashed another potion, which landed on Poppy's glasses and clouded her vision.

"I can't see," Poppy cried.

Veronica laughed, then screamed out, "Backup! I need you now."

Brett, Brian, Joe, and Poppy were shocked when a

group of people with green hair in ponytails emerged from the mine.

"This is my army." Veronica laughed as a second crop of husks marched from the mine and made their way toward the center of Sandy Vista.

"I have husks and people helping me. I will defeat you guys. There will be no Sandy Vista or Meadow Mews by the end of the week," said Veronica.

"We will stop you," said Brian. "You can't destroy our towns and hurt innocent people."

"Why not?" Veronica questioned.

"You're a bully," said Poppy as she sipped a potion to regain her strength.

"Maybe I am," said Veronica, "but I don't really care."

This comment infuriated Poppy, and she leaped at Veronica again, and this time she was able to strike Veronica and weaken her.

"You made me lose a heart." Veronica was upset. "You are going to pay for this."

Poppy slammed her sword into Veronica's shoulder, and Veronica lost a second heart. Veronica called out to the army, "Attack her!"

Four soldiers surrounded Poppy, and one said, "You are now our prisoner. We are putting you in the jail."

"No!" Poppy called out, but it was pointless. She couldn't battle the soldiers on her own, and her friends were in a battle of their own. Joe, Brian, and Brett were battling soldiers and Veronica. They were using all their energy to battle these criminals and make their way into the mine to deactivate the spawner. The trio was about to give up. They were losing energy, and they were concerned about Poppy. Brett called out, "Don't take Poppy."

One of the soldiers announced, "You guys are our prisoners," and they marched them inside.

"We failed everyone," said Brian. "We weren't even able to deactivate the spawner."

"We will find our way out, and we will deactivate the spawner," said Brett.

"I hope that's true," said Joe.

They were all tired and were losing hope. This battle had gone on too long, and they were worried that Veronica might win. Brett thought about Sandy Vista and how it had only lived in folktales. He feared that Meadow Mews might have a similar ending.

The soldiers walked the gang into the jail cell and locked the gate. Poppy stood with her hands resting on the bars. "How did we wind up here?"

The soldiers laughed as they walked down the dimly lit dirt hallway.

"It doesn't matter how we got here," said Brett. "All we have to do is concentrate on how to get out."

"That's easier said than done," Poppy remarked. "We came here to deactivate a spawner, and we couldn't even do that. Perhaps Veronica is just much stronger than us, and we have no way of defeating her."

"We can't have that kind of attitude, or we will never survive. We have to come up with a plan," said Brett.

"I like the way you think," a voice called out from the corner of the dark jail cell.

"Who said that?" asked Brett.

Joe pulled a torch from his inventory and explored the dark, musty jail cell. Two red eyes peered up at him, and he grabbed his sword and struck the cave spider. As he annihilated the spider, he saw feet in the corner, and he looked up and saw a man with gray hair and a long beard.

"Who are you?" asked Joe.

"I'm Lyle."

"Lyle?" Brett was stunned. He walked toward the sound of Lyle's voice and asked, "Aren't you the founder of Sandy Vista? I've heard so many folktales about you. I thought you weren't real."

"Of course he's real," said Brian.

"Yes, I am," said Lyle. "And I can help you."

12

FOLKTALES

"How can you help us?" asked Joe.

Brian rushed to his side. "You are okay. I was worried about you." He told the others, "Lyle helped me deactivate the spawner. I thought Veronica destroyed him. She told me that we were on hardcore mode."

"Are we on hardcore mode now?" questioned Poppy.

"No," said Lyle, "she doesn't have us on hardcore mode. She did destroy me, but I just respawned, and when I did, she placed me in this jail cell."

"How can you help us?" Joe asked again.

"I've spent a lot of time down here, and I hear things," explained Lyle. "I know that Veronica's army isn't happy with her. We have to get them to admit how much they dislike her, and once we do that, we can use them to destroy her."

"Do you think that's a possibility? How can we get close to her army?" asked Poppy.

"I've been talking to the people she calls soldiers. She doesn't even know their names, and this upsets them. I know their names, and I ask them questions about themselves, and they seem to be very receptive to this behavior. Basically, I treat them like humans."

"You're just like they said in the folktales. You are supposed to be wise and a person who only thinks about others. You're also supposed to know the secrets to the Overworld and life."

Lyle laughed. "The secrets to life. There is no secret to life. I just live my life being kind to others, and I hope that people are kind to me. I want everyone to be happy. Of course, if you are hurting others, I will work tirelessly to stop you."

"You're so wise," said Poppy.

"Thank you," said Lyle. "Can I ask you guys a question? What type of folktales have you heard about me? And why are there tales about me when I am here?"

"This is going to sound strange," said Poppy, "but we're from the future."

"That doesn't sound strange at all. I have been able to time travel. I've fallen down portals and landed in the future."

"Then you know that people can't find Sandy Vista? That folks spend their lives trying to track down this famous desert town?" questioned Brett.

"I do." Lyle's eyes filled with tears. "But we will change that. I know once we defeat Veronica that

Sandy Vista won't be a lost city. It will be a vibrant town that will survive in the Overworld."

"We want to help you," said Brett.

Joe said, "Veronica is also trying to destroy another town. One that is in the future. It's called Meadow Mews."

"Yes," said Lyle, "I know, and that's awful."

"We have to stop her," said Brian.

"We will," said Lyle. "But first I just want to hear one folktale about me. I am just curious to hear what stories are important enough to be retold and turned into legends."

"There's one that everyone in the Overworld knows," said Brett. "It involves you crafting a farm in the desert when nobody believed it was possible to build one."

"Yes." Lyle smiled. "That was when the Overworld was first created, and people didn't believe farms could be built in the desert. Now we know they can be, and they can flourish."

"I'm a farmer," said Brett.

"So am I," added Joe.

"I am so happy to meet fellow farmers," said Lyle. "I'm also glad that one of those folktales tells about my love of farming."

"Do you really think you can get us out of here and help us defeat Veronica?" asked Brian.

"I hope so," said Lyle. "I can't promise anything, but I will work my hardest to defeat her. I hope one day our battle against Veronica will become a famous folktale."

"Me too," said Poppy.

One of the soldiers arrived and stood by the gate. "Lyle," the green-haired soldier called out.

"Yes, Ruby is that you?" Lyle asked.

"It is." She smiled as she stood by the bars. "I brought you a piece of cake. Veronica would be so mad if she knew I took a piece for you. She just made us have a party to celebrate putting more people in jail. I didn't eat my slice, but I saved it for you."

"Thank you," Lyle said, "but I can't take your slice of cake. It's yours."

"No, I want you to have it," Ruby insisted.

"I have an idea." Lyle smiled as he made his way toward the gate. "Why don't we split it?"

"That sounds like a great idea," Ruby said as she cut the cake in two, "but what about the others? Will they be mad?"

"No," said Lyle. "They actually want to ask you a favor."

"Really?" asked Ruby as she handed the slice to Lyle. He took a bite.

Brett walked toward the gate. "Ruby, we wanted to ask you if you can help us stop this battle. We don't want to battle Veronica."

"I'm in." She smiled as she finished the cake.

13

SPIDERS AND SKELETONS

"**R**eally? That's awesome!" Brett exclaimed.

"I want to stop Veronica and so do my friends. We don't want to be her soldiers," confessed Ruby. "But how?"

Lyle asked, "How many of you want to stop Veronica?"

"I know my two good friends also want to stop her," Ruby replied.

"Find your friends and bring them here, and we will start to plan," said Lyle.

"Plan what?" a voice boomed.

Ruby turned around and screamed, "Veronica!"

"Yes," Veronica said. "Soldier, I am here, and I know you guys are planning something. How can you work with these people? Now I will have to place you in jail alongside them."

Ruby grabbed her diamond sword and swung it at

Veronica, slicing into her arm, but Veronica splashed a potion of weakness on Ruby. Ruby felt a wave of fatigue, and Veronica used this opportunity to put Ruby in jail.

"You guys are never going to get out," warned Veronica, "and I will find out who your traitor friends are, and I will stop them. Nobody will defeat me."

Veronica left, and the gang stood in the dark jail cell. Joe was the first to speak. "What are we going to do next? Does anybody have a plan?"

"We will stick to the original plan," said Lyle.

"How?" questioned Brett. "We have Ruby in here, and Veronica knows what we were planning. Let's just face it: we're trapped, and it's over."

"You can't talk like that," said Lyle. "You have to believe that we can still save Sandy Vista."

Brett wondered if Lyle was the reason Sandy Vista was a lost city. Perhaps he had ideas that things could change, but they were just dreams. Maybe Lyle didn't know how to come up with a good plan of action and stick with it. Brett thought about all of the situations he had experienced in the past and how many times he had thought he had no chance of escape. Somehow there was always a way out. Thinking about this reassured Brett that there was still hope. However, when he heard a loud explosion and the roof of the stronghold fell down on top of them, he wondered if they would be crushed and his hope began to vanish.

"Help!" cried Ruby as chunks of the roof rained down on them. Dirt got into everyone's eyes, and they couldn't see.

"What's happening?" asked Poppy. Her glasses were covered in dirt and dust.

"I think something exploded," said Brian.

"But why?" asked Poppy.

A familiar voice called out in the distance, "Brett? Joe? Poppy? Are you there?" Smoke filled the dimly lit jail cell as the voice grew louder. "Guys, where are you?"

"Nancy?" Brett could barely speak. His lungs were full of smoke, and he began to cough.

"Yes," Nancy replied. "I'm here with Helen. We're going to rescue you guys, but we have to do it fast because Veronica is after us."

"But we can't see," explained Poppy as she coughed.

"Just keep talking, and we'll find you," Nancy reassured her.

"Your voice is getting louder," said Helen. "We are getting closer."

Smoke surrounded them, and they couldn't see. When the smoke began to clear, the only thing Brett could see were two large red eyes staring at him.

"Guys! Spiders!" He smacked the spider with his diamond sword, but there was an endless amount of spider eyes surrounding him.

"We'll help you destroy the spiders. We see them too," said Nancy.

As the gang tried to destroy the spiders, Brett felt a stinging pain radiate down his arm. He turned around to see two skeletons aiming their bows and arrows at the gang.

"We don't have the energy to battle skeletons," said

Brett weakly. He had one heart left, leaving him incredibly vulnerable.

Nancy rushed toward Brett and handed him a potion of strength, which he drank quickly. With a renewed energy, Brett battled the skeletons and spiders.

"We have to get out of here," ordered Helen.

"I still can't see," Poppy explained.

"We will lead you out of here," said Nancy.

Brett, Brian, Joe, Poppy, Ruby, and Lyle followed Nancy and Helen out of the smoky prison and up the stairs and into the mine. When they were steps from exiting the mine, Veronica appeared in front of them.

"Where do you think you guys are going?" Veronica pointed her diamond sword at the gang.

"You don't scare us," said Nancy. "We are leaving."

"I believe you have something that belongs to me." Veronica pointed to Ruby.

"You don't own me," exclaimed Ruby.

"You're my soldier. I know now you think you have people who will back you up, but I created you, and you are mine," said Veronica.

"You can't own people," declared Helen.

"Ruby is free to go with us," said Lyle.

"No, she's not, Lyle," Veronica shouted and splashed a potion on Lyle that was so powerful that it destroyed him.

Brett remembered what Lyle had said about being on hardcore mode. He screamed out in anger, "What did you do to Lyle? Is he on hardcore mode?"

"Maybe," Veronica said and laughed.

Nancy was infuriated. She slammed her diamond sword into Veronica's unarmored shoulder, and Helen splashed a potion on her face. Veronica was left with one heart. Brett leaped at Veronica and delivered the fatal blow. When Veronica was destroyed, they bolted out of the mine and toward Sandy Vista.

"We have to find out if Lyle is still alive," said Brett.

The group didn't stop until they reached the desert temple. Queen Gail and King Jed stood outside. "You're back. I guess you guys destroyed the spawner. The husks are gone."

"We blew it up," said Nancy.

"It was intense," said Helen.

Brett said, "When we were in jail in the stronghold, we met a person you might know. His name is Lyle."

"Lyle is one of our best friends," said Queen Gail.

"I think Veronica destroyed him forever." Brett felt a lump in his throat as he said those words.

"Don't worry," a familiar voice called out. "I'm right here."

14

STRONG POTIONS

"Lyle." Brett let out a sigh of relief. "We thought you were destroyed."

"Thankfully, she didn't put me on hardcore mode," Lyle said.

"I'm so glad you're okay," said Brett. "I'm going to teach you how to brew potions so we can battle Veronica."

"Great," Queen Gail exclaimed. "I think this will help us a lot. Let's start now." But Queen Gail's smile turned to a frown when she saw a woman with a green ponytail walking behind Brett. "Who is she? She looks like the enemy."

"Her name is Ruby," Brett said. "She's on our side."

"How can we trust her?" King Jed questioned. "She is dressed like one of Veronica's soldiers. They were awful to me when I was being held prisoner."

"That wasn't me," Ruby said. "When you were

being held prisoner, I was working with my friends to overthrow Veronica. Now that Veronica knows this, she put me in the prison."

"This could be a trick," said Queen Gail. "A way that Veronica can spy on us."

Lyle said, "No, I don't think it's a trick. I believe Ruby. She wants to stage a revolt against Veronica. If we don't get Veronica's soldiers on our side, we will have an even tougher battle to fight. We have to believe her."

"Are we going to let her know the secret to brewing potions?" asked Queen Gail.

"Yes," said Lyle. "She is one of us now, and we have to treat her like everyone else here. She will learn to brew potions, and she will fight alongside us when we battle Veronica."

"I will prove that I'm a good warrior," said Ruby.

"I know you will." Brett smiled.

Callie went to the brewing stand that she had left in the temple and pulled out ingredients she had collected from the Nether. She held a ghast tear and placed it in an awkward potion. "This is now a potion of regeneration."

King Jed marveled. "Wow, we should all learn how to craft a brewing stand."

"You have to mine for the materials for a brewing stand," explained Callie. "Are there any mines near here?"

"We blew up the mine where Veronica trapped everyone," said Nancy.

"There must be more mines," said Callie.

"I'm afraid I don't know of any other mines," said Queen Gail.

"Me neither," Lyle said, "and I've been here a long time. We only used that mine."

"We will have to search for one. I saw mountains in the distance. There are always lots of mines and caves in the mountainous biomes," said Brett.

"Is this the time to travel all the way to the mountainous biome? We have to stay here and defend Sandy Vista," said Colin.

"Show us how to brew more potions," Jacques called out.

Callie stood by the brewing stand and taught them how to brew all sorts of potions and handed them out to the group. "Now we'll be prepared when Veronica returns."

A voice called out from the entrance, "You think knowing how to brew a potion will stop me?"

Veronica laughed as a group of soldiers trailed behind her. They carried diamond swords and bows and arrows. Ruby looked through the group for her friends, but she didn't see them. Veronica noticed Ruby eyeing her gang. "If you're looking for your traitor friends, they are gone. I have destroyed them."

"Destroyed them? You mean on hardcore mode?" Ruby's voice shook.

Before Veronica could respond, the soldiers leaped at the group. They struck the king and queen with their diamond swords and arrows. King Jed was destroyed, and Queen Gail screamed out in horror. Everyone was fearful that Veronica had set the world on hardcore mode. When King Jed respawned in the temple, the gang was relieved. Yes, they had to battle Veronica, but at least the stakes weren't as high as they had believed.

Colin and Jacques were excited to use the potions they had brewed with Callie. Jacques splashed a potion of harming on Veronica, but she quickly swallowed a potion to regain her strength. "Looks like you're an expert on how to brew potions now. That isn't going to help you. I have you outnumbered."

The gang let out a collective gasp when they saw another crop of soldiers entering the temple, and they wondered how many more soldiers Veronica had created. They used their swords and potions to battle them, but as they struck the green-haired, ponytailed soldiers, another army of a different sort entered the temple.

"Husks!" Brett screamed.

A line of husks flooded the entranceway, and the gang didn't know which battle to fight. Should they fight Veronica's soldiers or the husks? They didn't have time to decide because the husks grabbed both the gang and the soldiers, inflicting them with an intense hunger.

A husk struck Brett, and his stomach began to growl. He wanted to sprint from the temple and into the farm and fill his belly with apples and potatoes. His blond hair waved as he leaped at the husk that had attacked him and destroyed the desert beast.

Poppy was surrounded. She had a husk behind her and one of Veronica's soldiers in front of her. Skillfully using her diamond sword, she slammed her weapon into the soldier and the husk, destroying both. The victory was short-lived, because within seconds she was battling another soldier and another husk.

Veronica and her soldiers were annoyed. They didn't want to battle the creatures they had spawned to destroy the residents of Sandy Vista. As Veronica slew a husk, she was angry with herself for creating this invasion. The husk attack was her fault.

However, as she struck and destroyed another husk, Veronica remembered that the spawner she had created wasn't working anymore. She had watched Nancy and Helen blow it up. She realized that she didn't know where these husks were coming from. Was the spawner somehow reactivated? Had one of her soldiers fixed the spawner? This seemed impossible because it wasn't easy to construct the original spawner, and to build it they needed a few soldiers and more command blocks, which she didn't have.

Veronica looked over at one of her soldiers battling alongside her. "The husks," she said, but her voice was weak, and she could barely get a sound out.

"What about the husks?" the soldier questioned.

She remembered the mine from which they were operating was destroyed. Had one of her soldiers found a new place to create a spawner? Was her army that well trained? Did they have supplies she didn't know about? Or was there another criminal in their midst?

15

THE RETURN OF THE HUSKS

The sound of growling stomachs was heard through the battle as they all felt an intense collective hunger. Brett didn't think he could swing his diamond sword at another husk unless he ate something. He looked over at his friends. He wanted to suggest that they take a break and eat some food, but he knew there was no time to stop battling the husks.

Brian called out, "We have to find out where the new spawner is and deactivate it."

Nancy looked over at Veronica. She was in the middle of battling a husk. Nancy thought it was ironic that Veronica and her army were forced to battle these hostile mobs that they had spawned. There was no escaping these powerful mobs. Veronica was slamming her sword into the belly of a husk when Nancy confronted her.

"Tell us where the spawner is located. Even you are losing energy battling these mobs," said Nancy.

Veronica destroyed the husk. She wanted to tell Nancy that she had no idea where the spawner was located and this attack had nothing to do with her or her army, but she didn't want Nancy knowing that information because it would make her look weak. Instead of responding, Veronica swung her sword at Nancy, who backed away from the strike.

"What is wrong with you?" screamed Nancy. "Stop this attack now!"

Veronica hollered, "Never!"

The husks continued to march into Sandy Vista, and the gang was tired. They weren't going to last unless they got food. Jacques was the first one to say, "We need food, and I am going to get it for everyone."

"How?" King Jed questioned as two husks surrounded him. He swung his sword at one while the second attacked him. His voice was faint as he said, "We need every person battling these beasts."

Jacques slammed his sword into the husk that attacked the king. "If I don't get apples for everyone, we will all be destroyed."

"He's right," said Queen Gail. "Go get us apples."

Colin and Jacques dashed toward the farm and battled two husks that stood by the entrance to the Sandy Vista Farm. Once they had destroyed the husks, they rushed into the farm and began picking apples. They ran back to the desert temple and began distributing them to the hungry fighters. As Jacques handed out the apples, one of Veronica's soldiers asked if she could have an apple. Jacques didn't know what to do. He knew she was hungry, but she was also his enemy. He couldn't hand her an apple.

"Please," she called out. Her voice was weak.

Jacques handed her an apple. "I can't see someone starve, but you have to remember that we are not your enemy. This is a battle that Veronica has staged on her own, and you have a choice if you want it to continue."

"Thank you," the soldier replied. She took a bite of the apple.

A husk leaped at Jacques as he struck the beast and destroyed it. He looked out in the distance and saw a new group of husks making its way through the desert. Brian called out to Jacques, "Does it look like they are coming from the direction of the mountainous biome?"

"Yes," said Jacques.

"Then I have to go there. We won't be able to stop the invasion if we don't stop the spawner," said Brian.

"I will go with you," said Poppy.

"Me too," added Brett.

Veronica watched as the trio made their way toward the mountainous biome, and when they were out of view, she sprinted in their direction. She didn't alert any of her soldiers. She just quietly exited the temple and trailed behind them.

Poppy felt somebody following them. She wanted to stop and look back. But they were steps from a large mountain, and Brian had located an entrance to a cave. "I think the husks are coming from here!"

Husks were walking out of the entrance to the cave. One of the husks leaped at Brian, and he pierced the beast with his enchanted diamond sword, destroying it. He raced inside the dark cave as Brett pulled a torch from his inventory to help them see.

"Watch out!" Poppy cried as she saw a pair of red eyes staring at them.

"It's just a spider," said Brian as he destroyed the arachnid. "We have bigger issues. We have to find the spawner."

Two more spiders crawled toward them. Poppy slammed her sword at the spiders. She looked down at the ground. "Silverfish!"

The ground was filled with silverfish. Brian said, "Just run over them. We can't waste our time with insects."

The silverfish nibbled at their feet, destroying their energy. The gang shared a potion of healing to combat the attack from the silverfish as they made their way into the cave in search of the spawner.

Brett clutched the torch. "It looks like it might be down this hall." He flashed it down the hall as he tried to avoid the husks that marched down the narrow path.

Poppy raced ahead. "It is! I see it!"

"We have to destroy it," ordered Brett.

The gang pulled their pickaxes from their inventories and began to break the spawner into pieces. After a few strikes, the spawner deactivated.

"We did it!" exclaimed Brian.

"Good job," a cold voice called out from the corner of the cave.

"Veronica, did you follow us here?" questioned Poppy.

"Does it matter?" asked Veronica.

"Why are you building all of these monster spawners? You are terrible," said Brian.

"I want to destroy you," she replied.

Behind Veronica a deep voice called out, "Don't take credit for something you didn't do."

The group was stunned when a man wearing a red jumpsuit and dark sunglasses appeared. Brett asked, "Who are you?"

"I'm the one who created the spawner," he replied.

"Is this true?" Brian asked Veronica.

She didn't reply. She simply splashed a potion on her body and disappeared.

16

NEW PLANS

"Who are you?" asked Brett.

"I'm Ron," he introduced himself, "and I want to apologize for creating the husk spawner. I actually believed this part of the Overworld was empty and didn't have any inhabitants."

"Why did you craft a spawner?" asked Brian.

"I'm new to the Overworld, and I was teaching myself how to craft monster spawners. I'm trying to acquire the skills to survive. I just learned how to build a house, and now I am going to mine for materials for a brewing stand," Ron explained.

"I need to do that too," said Brian.

"Let's do it now," suggested Ron.

Poppy reminded them about the silverfish that lined the floor of the cave. "We have to destroy these silverfish. They are making us lose energy."

"Yes," said Ron, "we must." Ron slammed his sword at the ground, destroying groups of silverfish.

As they made their way toward the area where they could mine, Ron asked them, "Where are you guys from?"

"Different places," said Brian. "I'm from Sandy Vista."

"Where is that?" asked Ron.

"It's not far from here, but it's under attack," said Brian.

"I assume your town is being attacked by the woman who tried to take credit for my spawner, right?"

"Yes," replied Brian. "She is vicious."

"Why does she want to attack your town?" asked Ron.

"Since you're new to the Overworld, we don't want to jade your view of life here, but there are many grief-ers who only exist to destroy your property. Veronica wants to be known for destroying towns. I know it doesn't make sense, but these things never made sense to me," said Brett.

"I've met people like that before, which is why I was learning how to create a spawner. I want to be strong," explained Ron.

"Learning how to build a monster spawner doesn't make you strong," said Poppy.

"Really? Why not?" asked Ron as he destroyed another silverfish that crawled on the ground.

"You need to build friendships and help people. That's what makes you strong. You don't teach yourself how to craft spawners that create mobs that can hurt other players. I think that's the opposite of becoming strong," said Poppy. She added, "But that's just my opinion."

The final silverfish was destroyed, and Brian said, "I agree with you Poppy, but we don't have time to debate who and what is strong. At this moment Veronica can be destroying Sandy Vista."

"And Meadow Mews," Brett reminded them.

Brian said, "We should mine for materials and brewing stands quickly so we all have them and can craft potions to battle Veronica."

"I agree," said Brett. "If we can find them quickly, we should obtain them." Brett climbed into the hole in the mine and banged his pickaxe against the blocky ground. Within a few minutes he unearthed materials for a brewing stand and pulled them from the mine.

"Wow," said Poppy. "Are there any other ones?" She climbed into the hole next to Brett and began to mine for more brewing stand materials.

As the gang mined for materials for brewing stands, Nancy and Helen rushed into the mine and said, "There you guys are!"

"Is Sandy Vista under attack again?" asked Brian.

"Again?" Nancy was surprised. "The attack never stopped. It has been going on forever. After the husks were destroyed, Veronica had her army trap everyone in the desert temple. We were able to escape. You have to come back and help us save everyone."

"Hi." Ron looked up from the mine. "I'm Ron. I will help you guys."

"Thanks. We need all the help we can get," said Nancy.

Helen pulled her red hair from her face. "I think we should go right now."

"Can we wait a second? We just found materials to make brewing stands. This will strengthen our people, and we can battle Veronica," said Brian.

Ron said, "I thought Poppy said that strength was helping other people and being a good friend. We don't need these materials for brewing stands if your friends are in jail. We have to free them from Veronica."

"I like the way you think," said Nancy.

"Me too." Poppy blushed.

The gang was about to exit the cave when a cold wind blew through it. "What was that?" questioned Brian.

Brett had only felt that feeling of extreme cold when he was near a portal. He paused and saw a hole in the ground next to the cave's exit. He walked over and inspected it. "There's a portal!"

"What's that?" questioned Ron.

"If you jump in, you are transported to another point in time," said Brett.

Poppy looked at the portal. She wanted to jump in. She wanted to be transported back to her life in Meadow Mews, but she knew that she couldn't abandon her friends. She stood and stared at the hole.

"We have to go," said Brian.

"Poppy," Nancy said, "you aren't considering going down that hole, are you?"

"Maybe one of us should go back to see if Meadow Mews is okay. We should find out if Veronica destroyed it."

"Poppy," said Nancy, "we can't."

Helen stood next to Poppy. "But what if we never see another portal again?" questioned Helen. "What if we can never go back home?"

"We miss our home a lot," added Poppy.

"I know we do," said Brett, "but I've had to make this sort of choice before, and I'm telling you that if you go down that hole, you will regret it. You have to help the folks at Sandy Vista. We can't abandon them."

Poppy inhaled the cold air from the portal. If she just hopped inside this portal, this would all be over. There wouldn't be any more husk attacks, and she wouldn't have to battle Veronica and her army in Sandy Vista. She could concentrate on saving Meadow Mews and stopping Veronica if she had soldiers attacking their town too. She looked over at Brian, who stood right outside the cave. She stared at the portal and then walked toward Brian. She hoped she was making the right decision.

17

DESERT DUEL

"**Y**ou made the right choice," Brett told Poppy. "You'll see."

The gang sped toward the desert temple. As they approached the grand structure, they saw Queen Gail and Veronica standing across from each other. They weren't dressed in armor, but they clutched diamond swords. Everyone surrounded them, as if they were about to stage a play. Brett called out, "What's happening?"

Colin replied, "There's going to be a duel."

"What? A duel between Queen Gail and Veronica?" Brett questioned.

Veronica answered, "Yes, we will duel. We are unarmored and on hardcore mode. We are dueling to the end. If I win, I will be the ruler of both Sandy Vista and Meadow Mews."

"Why do you have to be on hardcore mode?" asked

Poppy. "That seems rather intense. Why can't one of you just know you're the loser and one is the winner? Why does it have to be the end of one of you?"

Veronica eyed Queen Gail and wondered if she might be stronger or a better fighter and if this might be the end of her. She said, "Maybe you're right. Perhaps we shouldn't do this on hardcore mode."

Everyone was shocked when Veronica said these words. Veronica ordered one of the soldiers to destroy the command blocks before the duel proceeded.

Poppy said, "Thank you. I am glad you came to your senses."

The soldier came back and announced the command blocks were destroyed.

Jacques asked everyone to give Queen Gail and Veronica space as he announced that the duel was about to begin.

"The duel will begin after I count to ten," announced Jacques. His voice shook, he was nervous, and he feared that Queen Gail would be defeated and they would spend their lives under Veronica's rule. He wondered if she'd want to wear Queen Gail's crown. He hoped Veronica wouldn't win. Life would be unbearable if she did. He began to count to ten. His voice cracked when he reached nine, and he felt like he was about to faint when he said, "Ten. It has begun."

Queen Gail's heart raced. She had never been in a duel, and she wasn't a skilled fighter, but she knew that the fate of Sandy Vista depended on her winning this duel. Queen Gail looked over at Nancy, who smiled at her. She remembered how scared she was in the Nether and how Nancy had taught her to battle a ghast. She knew that she could do things that she was afraid of and that she was stronger than she believed. Despite all of these thoughts, she was still frightfully nervous about partaking in a duel.

Veronica sprinted toward Queen Gail, but the queen stopped her. Queen Gail was the first to swing her sword at Veronica, slicing into her arm. Veronica cried out in pain but quickly stifled her cries because she didn't want to appear weak. Veronica leaped at Queen Gail, but Queen Gail dodged the strike and lunged at Veronica.

"Ouch!" Veronica cried as tears streamed down her face. She wanted to wipe them, but she couldn't let go of her diamond sword. Veronica took a deep breath, leaped at Queen Gail, and struck the queen's arm with her diamond sword. Veronica was confident after getting one strike in, and she hoped that she'd be able to defeat Queen Gail.

Veronica slammed her sword into Queen Gail two more times, leaving her with only two hearts, and Queen Gail was beginning to worry that this was the end. Queen Gail used all of her energy to pierce Veronica's belly, which left Veronica with two hearts. The duel was tied. They were both equally weakened. Queen Gail swung her sword at Veronica, and Veronica tripped and dropped her sword.

"Oh no!" Veronica said. "My sword."

Queen Gail stood above Veronica as she slammed

her sword into Veronica's arm, leaving her with one heart. Queen Gail looked at Veronica and said, "I don't have to destroy you. You have no weapon. It would be cruel to destroy you. I want you to know that you have caused a lot of trouble in our town, and you need to understand that your actions have hurt a lot of people."

"You don't want to destroy me and be declared the winner?" asked Veronica. She was weak and weaponless and confused.

"No, I don't get satisfaction out of destroying other people," said Queen Gail. "I get it by helping people. I'd rather have you promise that you have changed and that you will become an active member of our community than simply destroy you and know that I have won."

Veronica was surprised by this reaction. She couldn't imagine not destroying someone when you had the chance, but as she listened to Queen Gail talk, she tried to make sense of her logic. "You will let me live and stay here if I promise not to attack you. You mean you would end this duel and walk away with not winning?"

"Yes," Queen Gail said. "Winning and losing aren't as important as how we can change the way we view each other. I don't want you to be our enemy and I want you to be able to live here and not destroy Sandy Vista."

"You want me to stay here?" questioned Veronica. "Nobody ever wanted me to stay in their town before."

"That's because you were probably attacking the town," said Queen Gail.

"That's true," said Veronica.

"I know you have the capacity to change. Will you try, and we can end this duel?" asked the queen.

Veronica put out her hand and said, "Yes, I will try."

Queen Gail picked up Veronica's diamond sword and handed it to her. "You can take this back. I know you won't attack me with it."

Veronica smiled and placed the sword back in her inventory. "Thanks for letting me stay."

Ruby walked over to Veronica. "Can we be free from your army?"

"Yes, Ruby," said Veronica.

"You know my name?" Ruby was shocked.

"I know all of your names," confessed Veronica.

"We should have a celebration," said King Jed. "We will host a large feast tonight."

"Can I come?" asked Ron.

Brian said, "Yes, and you can stay in Sandy Vista."

"Everyone can stay in Sandy Vista," declared King Jed, and there was a loud cheer amongst the group.

Helen and Nancy looked over at the other folks from Meadow Mews. Nancy said, "I'm afraid we can't stay. We have to go back to Meadow Mews, but we don't know how to get back there."

"We saw a portal," exclaimed Poppy. "Maybe it's still active."

"Where?" asked Nancy.

"In the mountainous biome," said Poppy.

"We have to go there," said Nancy.

Queen Gail asked, "You're going to leave us?"

"I'm sorry," said Brett. "We have to get back home. But if you want to see us off, you should go to the mountainous biome with us, because you can mine for materials for brewing stands there."

Queen Gail said, "It will be heartbreaking to say goodbye to you, but we know you need to leave and go home. Let's go to the portal."

The entire town hurried toward the mountainous biome and the cave where they had seen the portal. As they traveled there, Poppy hoped the portal was still active. She would be so disappointed if the portal wasn't there. As they approached the cave, she felt the cold air, and her heart raced with excitement.

"We're going home," she said with a smile.

18

PRACTICAL JOKES

Poppy stood beside the portal. Brett looked over at her. "Now is the right time to go home."

"I know," said Poppy.

She was the first to jump in. Her glasses froze in the cold air, and she fell through the portal. Brett followed behind Poppy, and he could see the top of her head as he traveled through the portal. He could see her braids flying through the windy tunnel. It felt as if they were traveling forever when they landed in the middle of Meadow Mews.

"We're home," exclaimed Poppy as her friends landed around her. She looked at Joe. "So who won the contest?"

Joe laughed. "I don't even know what pranks were pulled."

"We must have a feast and go over all the pranks, and you can decide," said Poppy.

The sun was shining, and Brett suggested they all pick food from the farm and hunt for chickens and meat so they could have the ultimate feast that night. Poppy suggested that she bake cakes and cookies.

"Let's meet at my house before sunset," said Poppy, "and we can start the feast."

The gang spent the day preparing for the feast. They were all glad to be back in Meadow Mews and in their time period. They were also happy that Veronica had stopped trying to destroy Meadow Mews. When they had all gathered their supplies, they met at Poppy's house and began the feast.

As they dined on this decadent meal, Brett suggested, "We should plan a trip to Sandy Vista. I wonder how everyone is doing there. I miss them all."

"Yes," said Helen. "We should plan a trip. Now that Sandy Vista isn't a lost city anymore, it would be nice to visit and see our friends."

"I wonder how Veronica is and if she has truly changed," said Joe.

"I wonder," said Poppy, "who won the practical joke competition."

Joe laughed. "Okay, tell me your pranks. I have to say that the one Brett pulled on me was very funny." Joe explained how Brett splashed a potion of invisibility on himself and then removed crops while Joe was farming.

"That is funny," said Nancy.

"As you guys know, I was able to see it. I was cracking up," said Poppy.

The group talked about all of their pranks, and Joe laughed when he heard about each of them. "Did you seriously fill her house with chickens?" He laughed.

"So who is the winner?" asked Poppy.

"Does it matter who won?" asked Joe. "Wasn't the fun in planning the pranks and being pranked?"

Poppy thought about what Queen Gail said during the duel. It really didn't matter who was the winner or loser. She knew that the practical joke competition was fun. Everyone enjoyed it, and that should be her reward. She was the one who came up with the idea for the competition, and she had made her friends happy.

Poppy said, "I want to declare that we are all winners. Can I do that, Joe?"

"Of course." Joe smiled. "As you guys know, I am not a fan of being pranked, but I actually had a lot of fun during this competition. We should make this an annual tradition."

"We should," said Poppy.

The gang was ready for dessert, and Poppy handed out plates of cookies and cake. It was a well-earned dessert, and they enjoyed the cookies while they plotted the next year's practical joke competition.

"Maybe we should host it in Sandy Vista," suggested Callie.

"That sounds like a plan," said Poppy.

The sun was beginning to set, and Poppy suggested that everyone stay over at her house. They didn't want the party to end. They were busy talking about their upcoming trip to Sandy Vista.

"Thanks for talking me out of jumping down the portal before it was the right time," Poppy said to Brett.

"I'm glad you stuck it out," said Brett.

"Me too," said Poppy.

Poppy thought about returning to Sandy Vista and smiled. It was going to be a great competition next year. She was glad to have a lot of time to plan it.

The End